Slug Days

by SARA LEACH

Illustrations by Rebecca Bender

pajamapress

For my parents, Norm and Johanne
—S.L.

For Robyn, my butterfly girl
—R.B.

First published in paperback in Canada and the United States in 2020
First published in hardcover in Canada and the United States in 2017

www.pajamapress.ca   info@pajamapress.ca

Canada Council   Conseil des arts
for the Arts   du Canada

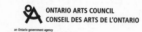
ONTARIO ARTS COUNCIL
CONSEIL DES ARTS DE L'ONTARIO
an Ontario government agency
un organisme du gouvernement de l'Ontario

Canadä

The publisher gratefully acknowledges the support of the Canada Council for the Arts and the Ontario Arts Council for its publishing program. We acknowledge the financial support of the Government of Canada through the Canada Book Fund (CBF) for our publishing activities.

Library and Archives Canada Cataloguing in Publication
Leach, Sara, 1971-, author
    Slug days / by Sara Leach ; with illustrations by Rebecca Bender.
ISBN 978-1-77278-022-2 (hardback).--ISBN 978-1-77278-032-1 (softcover)
    I. Bender, Rebecca, illustrator II. Title.
PS8623.E253S58 2017   jC813'.6   C2017-900643-6

**Original art created
with pencil
and digital media**

Publisher Cataloging-in-Publication Data (U.S.)
Names: Leach, Sara, 1971-, author. | Bender, Rebecca, 1980-, illustrator.
Title: Slug Days / by Sara Leach, with illustrations by Rebecca Bender.
Description: Toronto, Ontario, Canada: Pajama Press, 2017. | Summary: "Lauren, who has Autism Spectrum Disorder (an umbrella term that has included Asperger Syndrome since 2013), navigates the ups and downs of school and home life. School friendships have always been a challenge, but Lauren finds she is exactly the friend a brand new classmate needs" — Provided by publisher.
Identifiers: ISBN 978-1-77278-022-2 (hardcover) | 978-1-77278-032-1 (softcover)
Subjects: LCSH: Asperger's syndrome – Juvenile fiction. | Friendship – Juvenile fiction. | BISAC: JUVENILE FICTION / School & Education. | JUVENILE FICTION / Social Themes / Special Needs.
Classification: LCC PZ7.L433Slu |DDC [F] – dc23

Cover and book design—Rebecca Bender

Manufactured by Friesens
Printed in Canada

Pajama Press Inc.
181 Carlaw Ave. Suite 251 Toronto, Ontario Canada, M4M 2S1

Distributed in Canada by UTP Distribution
5201 Dufferin Street Toronto, Ontario Canada, M3H 5T8

Distributed in the U.S. by Ingram Publisher Services
1 Ingram Blvd. La Vergne, TN 37086, USA

As of the time
of this book's writing
and editorial process,
seat belts are not
required on school
buses in Canada or
in 44 US States. This
may change in the
future as lawmakers
continue to debate
the issue.

Chapter 1

I KNEW IT was going to be a slug day as soon as I climbed on the school bus. Mike wasn't there. The new driver didn't know our secret hand-shake. He didn't pretend to close the door before I was inside. He didn't know the front seat was reserved for me.

Dan and Sachi were sitting in my seat. I
squished between them.

"Hey!" Dan said. "Get out. Two to a seat, Lauren."

Mom told me when people look upset you should try to make them feel better. Dan had a frown on his face and he was using an angry voice, so I figured he must be upset. I gave him a kiss to make him feel better.

He pushed me.

I pushed him back.

He pushed me harder.

"Stop it!" Sachi said. "Lauren, go find another seat."

"No! This is my seat," I said.

"Brad!" Sachi called to the driver. "Make her move!"

The driver pulled the bus to the side of the road. He put out the red stop sign, turned on the flashing light, and turned to face me. "You're going to make everyone late for school. Find a new seat. Now."

Fine. I didn't want to sit with Dan and Sachi anyway. I stomped halfway down the bus and found an empty seat. I ignored the other kids. I didn't want to try to figure out what they were feeling.

I curled up in the corner of the seat and pressed my cheek against the cool metal of the side of the bus. Reaching into my pocket, I pulled out the squishy ball Dad gave me. He said I could bring it to school to help me cool down so I didn't flip my lid. He said that kids like me, kids with Autism Spectrum Disorder, didn't always see the world the same way as everyone else, and that I needed some special tricks up my sleeve. Mom said I had trouble "reading social cues," which meant I didn't understand what other people were feeling. She said the ball might help me when I "missed their social signals" and got into "difficult situations." Which meant not understanding what kids were thinking, and getting into fights.

I didn't keep the ball up my sleeve, but it did help sometimes. Usually I liked the way it slapped my fingers when I bounced it against my hand. But today, even the ball didn't make me feel better. Today was a slug day. On slug days, I felt slow and slimy. Everybody yelled at me. I had no friends.

Chapter 2

WHEN THE BUS arrived at school, I waited for everyone else to get off first. I didn't try to high-five Brad like I did with Mike most mornings. I felt jittery. Like something was missing from my day.

Instead of going down the metal stairs to the

playground like everyone else, I crawled under one of the pine trees that lined the school by the bus loop. The damp dirt and pinecones under me smelled like a good place for slugs. A good place for me. The tree made a tent above me. I bent my knees so my boots wouldn't stick out and give away my hiding spot. I liked the way the pine needles poked the palm of my hand. I tried wrapping my hand around a branch to see if I could get the tree to poke all five fingers at the same time.

The bell rang. I ignored it. It was already a slug day. Why make it worse by going in to class? Dan would push me again, and I'd get blamed for it. I poked the needles some more.

"Lauren? Are you out here?" Mrs. Kelly, the duty teacher, called my name over and over. I tucked my knees in tighter to keep my boots out of sight.

She saw me anyway. I heard her breathing near my tree, and saw the tips of her shoes as I peeked toward the parking lot.

"Lauren. The bell rang. It's time to go in. Stop wasting everyone's valuable time."

I sighed and scooched out from under the tree. I didn't know what the big deal was. There were two hundred kids and a whole bunch of teachers in the school, and she was only one adult. I wasn't wasting everybody's time. Just hers. If she didn't want to waste her time, she should stop looking for me.

She held my hand all the way downstairs to my classroom in room 163. Her hand was sweaty and warm, and kind of slippery. I tried to pull my hand away, because I wasn't a baby anymore, but she just gripped tighter. Like a Venus flytrap.

Chapter 3

"GOOD MORNING, LAUREN," Mrs. Patel said when Mrs. Kelly finally let go of my hand.

I wiped my hand on my skirt and walked to my hook. The custodian had put my gym bag on my hook again. He did it every night. I lifted the gym bag off the hook and put it on the floor. Then I put my jacket on the hook, followed by my backpack. I lined my boots up underneath my backpack and made sure they were centered. I pulled my shoes from their cubby and was tying them—I didn't like it when the bows were uneven—when Mrs. Patel came and stood beside me.

"Lauren, you've already missed ten minutes of reading because you were late. Please hurry."

I sighed. If she'd stop interrupting me, I'd get my bows done properly. Now I had to start all over again. When I had them perfect, I went to get my book for reading. Mrs. Patel chimed the bell. "Please put your books away, class, and return to your desks."

I wanted to slam my book on the counter. Reading time was one of my favorite parts of the day.

But I remembered the last time I'd done that. I slammed the book so hard, all the other books slid off the shelf. They landed on Abdel's head, and he had to go to the secretary to get some ice.

I had to go to the principal, and Mom and Dad were both there. Everyone told me again how I think differently from other kids and that's what makes me special, but I still have to be fair to my teacher and the other kids in the class. We had to make a plan for my safety and the safety of the kids in the class. I suggested maybe Abdel

shouldn't sit under a shelf of books. It probably wasn't safe, because we lived in an earthquake zone. And Mrs. Patel shouldn't make me stop reading until I was done. But the adults came up with a plan of their own. I'm not sure why they bothered bringing me to the meeting if they weren't going to listen to any of my suggestions.

Mrs. Patel must have remembered the plan, because before I could slam the book on the counter, she put a hand on my shoulder. "Here's your eraser," she said. "Squeeze it."

She gave me my favorite eraser, and I squeezed so hard my knuckles turned white. They looked like four mountaintops on my hand. Mrs. Patel must have taken the book from me, because when I stopped looking at the mountaintops, my other hand was empty.

Chapter 4

TUESDAY WAS A BUTTERFLY day. I didn't flip my lid at school once, and Mrs. Patel put a sticker in my agenda. That was my sixth sticker, which meant Mom took me to get ice cream.

Mrs. Patel thought I listened at school to get the sticker. Mom thought I listened to get the ice cream. They were both wrong.

When we arrived at the ice-cream store, I ran
to the counter. Mom thought I took a long time
deciding on my ice-cream choice because there
were so many flavors. She was wrong about that
too. I loved the ice-cream store because of the
goo on the counter.

There was a groove at the ice-cream counter where people's ice cream dripped and they couldn't clean it out. I ran my fingers through the gooey bits while I pretended to decide on a flavor. The bits were squishy and stretchy, like rubber bands. I loved to see how far I could stretch them.

"What's it going to be, Lauren?" Mom asked. "Cookie dough?"

"No," I said, pulling my fingers through the goo.

"Double-chocolate chip?"

I shook my head and moved down the counter, dragging my fingers in the groove.

"Time to decide," Mom said.

I moved another step down the counter, but this time my fingers stayed behind. "Uh oh," I said, tugging at them.

"What's wrong?" Mom asked.

"My fingers are stuck."

Mom closed her eyes and breathed in and out through her nose. Once I told her huffing like a bear wouldn't solve her problem. She didn't like that very much. "Pull harder," she said.

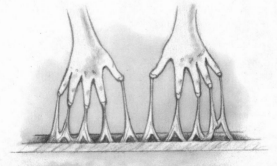

I tried. "They're still stuck." My insides started to go all wobbly. "What if I can't get them out?" I didn't want to live in the ice-cream store forever. It smelled good, and there weren't any teachers or mean kids, but I wouldn't be able to eat any ice cream because my fingers were stuck.

Mom yanked my arms. My fingers popped out of the groove. "Ow!" I yelled. But the hurt didn't last long. Long, stretchy gobs of pralines 'n cream dangled from my fingers.

"Pralines 'n cream it is," I said. "Two scoops."

Chapter 5

ON WEDNESDAY, AFTER I tied the bows
on my shoes, I reached inside my desk to feel the
sticky spot where my orange juice had spilled one
time. Every day the spot changed a little bit. The
day it spilled it was as sticky as slug slime. Each
day after that it felt dustier and more slippery.

But today all I felt was smooth, cold metal. I ran my hand on the other side of the desk. Maybe I'd made a mistake? No. I checked the outside of the desk. Maybe I'd sat in the wrong one? No, my

name was still taped to the front of it. I pushed my chair back and stuck my eye up to the inside of my desk. It was clean.

"The custodian cleaned my desk!" I called.

"Raise your hand, Lauren," Mrs. Patel said.

I raised my hand. "Someone cleaned my desk!"

Mrs. Patel pressed her lips together. "Wait until I call on you. That's a warning."

I clamped my hand over my mouth. Three warnings in a day meant no sticker in my agenda.

We did language arts until recess. I tried to
hurry and let my thoughts flow like Mrs. Patel wanted me to. I tried not to erase my words
too many times. But my g's and p's kept staying

above the line, and I knew they were supposed to dip below. I wasn't a baby anymore and didn't want my printing to look like a preschooler's, so I erased the words until I got them right. I erased one word three times, and my eraser made a hole in my paper.

I thought I might flip my lid, so I pulled out my squishy ball to help me calm down. It was part of my plan, and Mrs. Patel wasn't allowed to tell me to stop. Squishing the ball against my hand helped me feel better, so I did it some more. I started tossing it from hand to hand, because it felt really good when it landed. And then I started throwing it up in the air and catching it with both hands, because it felt good when it landed in both hands at the same time. And then I started saying, "Whoosh, whoosh," each time the squishy ball went up and down.

Mrs. Patel caught the ball when it was in the air.

"Hey! Give it back. The ball is part of my plan!"

Mrs. Patel took a deep breath. She looked right in my eyes. I looked around the room. The other kids were all staring at me too, so I looked back into her eyes.

"Squishing the ball is part of your plan. Throwing it is not. Can you make a good choice?"

I wanted to flip my lid and rip up my paper. Throwing the ball was a much better choice than that. Couldn't she see how grown-up and responsible I was being? Before I could explain, she asked again, "Can I trust you with the ball?"

"Yes."

She put it back on my desk and I grabbed it, but it didn't feel as good anymore.

"I wanna ball too!" Dan said. "How come I don't get a ball?"

Mrs. Patel stood up and pinched her nose between her fingers. She was like my mom that way. She thought it would make her feel better.

She needed her own squishy ball. "No, Daniel, you may not. Get back to your writing, please. The recess bell will be going soon."

By the time the bell rang, I had written two beautiful sentences. Mrs. Patel looked at them and sighed. "Your printing is lovely, Lauren, but I know you have a head full of great ideas. Why don't you try writing those ideas down?"

She didn't understand. I wanted to write them down, but those g's and p's kept getting in the way. I could have written a story with no g's or p's. But then I couldn't write about *going* anywhere or doin*g* anythin*g* and I couldn't write about *p*en*g*uins or do*g*s or ele*p*hants. And I didn't like cats.

Mrs. Patel didn't make me stay in at recess to write more today. I think she wanted to get upstairs and have a coffee with the other teachers.

Chapter 6

AFTER DINNER, DAD took the baby for a walk to get her to sleep.

Mom said, "The dishes can wait. You and I need to spend some time on Insectia."

Just like that, my day turned into a butterfly day. I ran to the craft closet and threw open the door. Mom slid Insectia off the top shelf and carried it with two hands to the kitchen table. I put the supply bin beside it.

"What should we work on tonight?" Mom asked.

I considered the question. We'd made pod houses for the caterpillars, a swimming pool for the water striders, and a spittlebug restaurant.

"Maybe we should make something for spiders?" Mom asked.

"Spiders aren't insects; they are arachnids. This is Insectia, not Arachnia."

"How about honeybees?" she asked. "They're insects. And important to have around."

I nodded. "Bees. But no wasps. They sting. And they don't make honey."

"I'm sure they have a purpose in our world," Mom said. "But I haven't figured out what it is yet."

"No wasps in Insectia. They don't have a purpose here." I pointed to an empty corner of our world. "The bees can live here."

"Will we build them hives?"

"Houses," I said. "Each room will be a hexagon. A hexagon has six sides. That is the shape of the cells inside a beehive."

I pulled a piece of cardboard and a box cutter out of the supply bin.

"What are the rules?" Mom asked.

I sighed. "Use the mat, watch my fingers, and close the knife when I'm done."

"Good. You may start."

Using the box cutter made me feel grown up, but I had to say the rules every time we worked on Insectia. Mrs. Patel never let me use a knife at school. Knives were not part of my safety plan. "How do I make a hexagon?"

Mom passed me a ruler. "Cut six pieces exactly the same size. I'll help you fit them together."

I worked on measuring while Mom took out the clay and began rolling pieces of yellow into little balls. That was how we worked—I built the houses and she built the insects. We made that plan after pieces of clay got stuck under my fingernails and made me itch, and my fingers bled because I picked them so much.

Mom looked at her watch. "We have forty-five minutes before it's time for bed."

I frowned. I didn't like bedtime. But I did like Mom telling me how much time we had. It was part of my safety plan at home. Mom gave me lots of warning, and then I didn't flip my lid when she told me time was up.

Chapter 7

FITTING THE HEXAGON pieces together was
hard. They didn't make perfect hexagon shapes the
way I wanted. Mom reached over to help me, but I
batted her hand away. I heard her huffing like a bear
again. I didn't want her to flip her lid and stop working
on Insectia, so I let her help me. When she held the

first two pieces together it was easier, and soon I had two bedrooms and a kitchen for the bees.

"You'd better get busy making those bees," I said. "I'll paint the house."

Dad came home with the baby just as Mom said, "Ten minutes left."

I didn't want to waste any time, so I didn't say anything to Dad.

He stood beside me. "What do you say when

someone comes into the room, Lauren?"

"Hello," I said.

"And where do you look?"

I breathed the way Mom does, put down my paintbrush, and looked at Dad. "Hello." I looked at the baby. "Hello." She was asleep in the front pack, with her legs dangling like two sausage links. She didn't answer me. I went back to painting.

"Eight minutes," Mom said.

"Nice hexagons," Dad said. "They are very regular."

"They aren't regular. They are special bee-house hexagons." I showed him my excellent black-and-yellow-stripes painting job.

Dad smiled. "Regular is a math word. It means the sides and angles are all the same."

"Oh," I said. "That's what I wanted. It was hard. Mom helped."

"Two minutes," Mom said.

I rushed to finish my painting and accidentally globbed black paint on the front of the bee kitchen. "No!" I cried. All my work was ruined. My face grew hot, and lava started to bubble and boil inside of me. I could feel angry steam filling my head.

Mom sucked in a deep breath like she was going to blow up a balloon.

My volcano was about to erupt. I opened my mouth to scream, and lifted the paintbrush to throw. Dad caught my arm and held it. "That's a nice door you just painted."

"What?"

"See?" He outlined the smear I'd made. It did look like a bee-sized door.

I nodded. The volcano cooled off. "I need to give it a doorknob." I dabbed a yellow dot on the smear.

Mom let out a big *whoosh* of air. "Cleanup time," she said.

Chapter 8

ON THURSDAY I went to see Ms. Lagorio
in room 272. She once told me her name meant
green lizard in Italian. It was a good thing she
was a very pretty lady. Imagine if she had old skin
and looked like a lizard.

When I arrived, she said we would be working on having conversations. We practiced where to stand when talking to a friend. She made me stand up and pretend to talk to her.

"Why do we need to practice this?" I asked. "I know how to talk to people."

"Sometimes other people don't like it if you stand too close to them," Ms. Lagorio said.

I didn't understand what she was talking about. I never stood too close to people.

Ms. Lagorio put her hands on my shoulders and nudged me backward a few steps. "That's a good distance to stand."

"But now I have to talk louder," I said in my outside voice.

Ms. Lagorio smiled. "No, honey. I can hear you just fine in your regular voice." She told me to hold my arm out straight. "That's how far you should stand."

After we practiced, she let me have a jelly bean because I listened so well, and she let me look at *Where's Waldo* for an extra ten minutes.

Chapter 9

WHEN I WENT back to the classroom, we did "Think, pair, share." Normally I didn't like it because it took me too long to think, and nobody wanted to pair and share with me. But I was excited to try the new arm-distance talking Ms. Lagorio had taught me.

Mrs. Patel said we should think about the province of Manitoba, which we have been studying. That was easy. I knew lots of facts about Manitoba. Like one time it was colder in Winnipeg than it was on Mars. And it is home to the largest den of garter snakes in the world. And Winnie-the-Pooh was named after a real bear that was named after Winnipeg.

I stopped thinking after three facts so I would be able to remember them when we paired and shared. I squeezed my eyes tight so the ideas wouldn't float out of my brain.

Mrs. Patel drew names to choose partners. She chose Dan and me to be together.

"No way!" Dan shouted.

Mrs. Patel stared at him until he muttered, "Fine."

I went to stand in front of him. I used what I learned from Ms. Lagorio and stretched out my hand until it touched Dan's shoulder.

"Don't touch me." Dan stepped back.

I moved forward and touched his shoulder again, so we would be the right distance apart.

"Quit it!" Dan said. He stepped back again. This time he backed into the bookshelf.

I stepped forward and measured the distance between us.

"If you touch me one more time, I'm going to punch your lights out," Dan said.

I dropped my arm. We were the right distance anyway. "I'll go first," I said.

"No. I'm going first."

"No, me!"

Mrs. Patel rushed over. "The person with the longest hair may go first," she announced to the class in a big voice.

Dan made his upset face again. I didn't kiss him to make him feel better. He looked too much like a lizard. Instead, I smiled and got ready to share my thinking. Except by then all the ideas had floated out of my head.

Chapter 10

FOR SNACK ON Thursday, Dad packed me
two hard-boiled eggs and a bag of crackers. My
favorite. I put the eggs in my skirt and crouched
on the ground beside my desk. "Bawk, bawk,"
I said, bobbing my head and bouncing up and
down. I looked just like a chicken. Alyssa started

laughing. So did Dan. Then I tipped forward, and the eggs rolled out of my skirt. "Look, I'm laying eggs!"

Alyssa started laughing even harder. Dan laughed so hard, milk sprayed out of his nose. Mrs. Patel didn't like that.

"Lauren! That's a warning. Give me those eggs and go back to your seat immediately!"

"But that's my snack," I said.

"They've been on the floor. And obviously you were more interested in playing with them than eating them." She walked to the compost bucket and dropped them inside. Right on top of Jackson's icky, mayonnaise-covered ham slice.

It was so unfair. Dan was the one who squirted milk out his nose. Why was I the only one who got in trouble?

I took my bag of crackers out of my lunch kit. Just before I started to smash the bag between my fingers to make dust, Mrs. Patel turned around and pointed a finger at me. "No dust."

I tried pinching the top of my nose to see if it would make the problem go away, but it didn't make me feel better at all. I didn't like eating crackers whole. I liked mushing them up and pouring the cracker dust into my mouth. Then I'd take a sip of water, and it would turn to cracker glue. I wished Mrs. Patel would stop making me have slug days.

Chapter 11

THURSDAY WAS PIZZA night. Pulling the cheese from my pizza with my teeth was almost as good as pulling the gooey ice cream out of the groove at the ice-cream store. Without the risk of getting my fingers stuck.

Dad made my pizza with extra cheese, even

though Mom said too much cheese wasn't good for me, and I should learn to eat it politely. Dad said pizza was finger food, so what difference did it make? And Mom huffed like a bear and fed the baby.

At the end of dinner, Dad said, "So what's it going to be, Lauren? Kitchen or baby?"

"Neither," I said.

Dad made a buzzer sound. "Wrong answer. Try again."

"You know the deal," Mom said. "We all help out on pizza night." She passed me an eraser.

I squeezed it tight. "Fine. Baby."

Mom's eyebrows shot up her forehead like two caterpillars that had just seen a fresh leaf. "Great! Would you like to read to her or give her a bath?"

"Read." Dad once told me the baby sometimes peed in the bathtub. I was not putting my hand in her pee.

Mom scooped the baby out of her high chair and brought her over to the couch. "You choose a book, Lauren."

I chose the shortest board book I could find. Mom plopped the baby right beside me. I scooted over. She crawled closer to me. I scooted over some more. The baby gurgled and put her hands on my shoulders. I tried to shake them off.

"Lauren," Mom said. "You'll hurt her. She's trying to see the book."

I put the book on the couch, and the baby squealed and tried to pick it up and eat it. I snatched it from her hands. It was covered in baby slime, which is not as sticky as slug slime or as stretchy as the goo at the ice-cream store. It is slippery and very gross. I went and took another book from the basket.

"You eat that one," I said. "I'll read this one."

"That's good problem solving," Mom said.

She could call it problem solving if she wanted. I called it staying dry. While the baby ate her book, I read the other one. I read fast, because I wanted to finish before she chewed her way through her book and came after mine.

"Slow down, honey," Mom said.

I sighed and read slower.

Chapter 12

I FINISHED THE book and snapped it shut. "Time for bed, Baby."

"That was pretty quick," Mom said. She handed me another book. "Read this one too."

Before I could say no, the baby saw the book and started clapping her hands and laughing.

Each page only had one word. And a big baby face. Since she wasn't trying to eat it, or me, I decided to read. Besides, it was short.

"Happy." I turned the page. "Sad." It was like the cards that Ms. Lagorio showed me when we talked about reading people's feelings. "Funny." I pretended to laugh like the picture of the little boy in the book. The real baby laughed with me. "Grumpy." I scrunched up my mouth like the girl in the picture. My real baby laughed.

"You're supposed to be grumpy," I said. But I didn't really care. When my baby laughed, it felt like butterflies fluttering around the room.

"Surprised." I lifted my eyebrows and opened my mouth like Ms. Lagorio taught me. My baby laughed and laughed. "That's the last page. Should we read it again?"

Lexi crawled onto my lap. And I let her.

Chapter 13

ON FRIDAY, MRS. Patel read us a story before lunch. I sat beside Alyssa on the carpet. I knew she liked me, because she laughed at my egg-laying yesterday. Mom said laughing with someone was a way of showing you liked them. So when I sat beside Alyssa, I sat really close. I

wanted to hug her, but Mom said not everybody
likes getting hugs, and sometimes I hug so tight I'm
like a boa constrictor. So I put my head in Alyssa's
lap and played with her hair instead.

But she must have had an itch, because she kept jerking away from me. I hoped she didn't have lice, because lice are a very big pain. They make your mom and dad really grumpy with all the laundry, and you have to sit very, very still and listen to audiobooks for hours and hours.

Thinking about lice made me worried, so I sat up and let go of her hair. "Good choice, Lauren," Mrs. Patel said. I wasn't sure if she meant sitting close to Alyssa, or not playing with her hair because of the lice thing.

I couldn't wait to go out at long recess and play with my best friend Alyssa. I ran to the cloakroom as soon as the bell rang, and pulled on my rain jacket. I didn't even want to take off my runners, but Mrs. Patel noticed and made me go back and get my boots. Then she saw me running down the hall, and I had to come back and practice walking to the door.

By the time I made it outside, Alyssa was already playing tag with Dan and Abdel and Sachi. "Who's it?" I yelled.

Nobody answered me, but it looked like Dan was it, so I ran away from him. When he didn't chase me, I ran toward him again. Then Alyssa was it. "Can't catch me!" I yelled. But Alyssa didn't chase me either.

"I'm it! I'm it!" I called. They all ignored me and ran to the playground. So I chased them over there. They played grounders, but they never let me be it. Then they ran to the basketball court. So I followed them there.

Alyssa turned at the edge of the court. "Stop following us, Lauren!"

I stopped. I thought she was my friend. I was wrong. It was a slug, slimy day. "Fine!" I yelled. "I don't want to play with you and your lice anyway!"

I ran and hid under my tree. Mrs. Kelly had to come find me and drag me back to class after long recess. Only this time, she didn't have to waste as much of her valuable time, because she knew where I was. Next time I'd have to find a better hiding place.

Chapter 14

WHEN I ENTERED the classroom after long recess, Mrs. Patel said, "I'm glad you're here, Lauren, because I have a surprise for the class."
I didn't like surprises. Especially not surprises by adults. Usually when an adult has a surprise, it's followed by them getting sad because you aren't

as happy with their surprise as they are. Like when Mom and Dad told me about the new baby. They had big eyes and smiles when they told me about the exciting change that was going to happen to our family. And then their faces turned all tight and frown-y when I said I didn't like change, and they could give the baby to another family. And they really didn't like it after the baby came home, and they had those big eyes again, and I asked if we could give the baby back to the nurses.

I didn't like change. They should have known that. Change meant I didn't know what was going to happen. Change made me feel jittery. Mrs. Patel knew that too. But there she was, smiling like a surprise was going to turn my day into a butterfly day.

"Everybody, we have a new student joining us today. Her name is Irma. I expect you to make her feel welcome."

There was a knock. "That will be her now." Mrs. Patel walked to the door.

So that was the big surprise? A new student? Maybe I could live with that change.

Mrs. Patel led Irma to the front of the class. "Irma is here from Sweden. She doesn't speak much English, so I need you to be extra helpful and kind." Mrs. Patel's eyes stayed fixed on Dan as she talked. "Say hello, class."

"Hello, Irma," we said.

"Hello, class," Dan said. Some of the boys started giggling. I wanted to laugh, but I decided to hide my smile behind my hand.

I needed to be kind and welcoming to Irma. And if I laughed with Dan, it would mean I liked him. Which I did not.

Chapter 15

MRS. PATEL LED Irma to the desk right behind mine. I stood up as she came by. I wanted to give her an extra-tight hug to welcome her to our class. But as I was about to, Mrs. Patel looked at me with eyeballs that said, *Stop.* So I sat down again and put my head on my desk and rolled my special eraser back and forth, smelling its straw-berry scent.

We started math. Two-digit subtraction. I didn't mind two-digit subtraction when Dad taught it to me. I liked numbers. I knew what to expect. And once you knew the steps, you could do two-digit subtraction exactly the same way each time and always get the right answer. But then Mrs. Patel decided she wanted us to figure out different ways to solve the problems, and we had to show her our thinking. And when I said I liked my way and it worked, she got mad. Now I spent most of math time feeling jittery and angry. I rolled my eraser a lot and did my math prob-lems at home with Dad, when he wasn't too busy with the baby.

Irma tapped me on the back. "Hello."

I turned to face her. "Hi." I remembered what
Mom taught me about introductions. I stuck out
my hand. "I'm Lauren."

Irma shook my hand. "I am Irma. How do
you do?"

I looked at her for a second. "How do I do what? Math?"

Irma tilted her head and looked at me. She nodded.

"I can't do this math anymore. Well, I can. But Mrs. Patel doesn't like my way. Would you like to squeeze my eraser?" I was trying very hard to be kind and welcoming. Mom says friends share things with each other.

"Thank you." Irma took my eraser and rubbed out her math question.

My mouth dropped open. She wasn't supposed to erase with my extra-special strawberry-scented eraser that rolled perfectly under my hand. I reached out to snatch my eraser back. But then Irma smiled at me.

I dropped my hand back on my desk. "You're welcome."

Chapter 16

WE HAD GYM at the end of the day. Gym is my slug-slimiest subject. Especially when we play dodgeball.

"We'll be playing dodgeball today," Mrs. Patel said. She split us into two groups. Irma and I were on the same team.

I showed her how to line up with a toe on the black line. "When Mrs. Patel blows the whistle, everyone runs and tries to get a ball from the center line. Then you throw it at people, but not their heads. If you get hit, you're out."

Irma nodded and smiled. She sure was a friendly girl.

The whistle blew. I charged for the center line and reached the ball just before Dan. I wrapped my hands around it from one side, and he wrapped his hands around it from the other. We played tug o' war for a few seconds.

"You're never going to win," he said. "You're a loser!"

I flipped my lid. I forgot all about my plan. I forgot about what Mom said about deep breathing. I stomped on Dan's foot hard, and he let go of the ball. "So there, Dan! I am NOT a loser!"

I threw the ball as hard as I could at him. It smacked him right on the shoulder, even though he tried to jump away.

"I got you!" I shouted.

Dan didn't sit down. He just grabbed my ball and ran toward me.

"I got you! I got you! You need to sit down!" I screeched so loud, Alyssa and Abdel covered their ears. I bet the man in the moon heard me. Dan didn't sit down. Then Noah threw the ball at me and hit me on the hip, and I had to sit down. Soon our whole team was sitting.

Mrs. Patel blew the whistle. "Team two wins this round," she called.

I jumped up and started yelling. "Dan cheated! Dan cheated!"

Mrs. Patel blew the whistle again. "Lauren, calm down, please."

"But he cheated!" It wasn't fair. AND I HATE LOSING! I ran for the bathroom and hid in the stall.

Chapter 17

MRS. PATEL FOLLOWED me into the bath-room. "No sticker for you today. You know that, right, Lauren?"

I plugged my ears to block out Mrs. Patel, but I still heard her sigh and clomp out the door. The bell rang. If I missed the bus, Dad could come and get me. So what if he had to wake the baby and waste his valuable time?

Somebody came into the bathroom. I unplugged my ears and heard sniffling. I poked my head under the stall and saw Irma. "Why are you sad?"

Irma wiped her face with her hands. "I am scared. Of the bus. I have nobody to sit on me."

"Nobody to sit on you? Why would you want that?"

"I want a friend."

"You mean you want somebody to sit *with* you? On the bus?"

Irma nodded.

"I'll sit with you."

Irma fiddled with her shoelaces. I ducked back into my stall and curled myself into a ball. A worm squiggled in my tummy while I waited.

She poked her head under the door. "Yes. I would like that."

The slug slime started to dry up, and I slid out of the cubicle. I wanted to hug her. But she might think I had lice, and twitch away.

Irma wrapped her arms around me. She felt like hot chocolate on a winter day.

"We better go quickly," I said. "We don't want to miss the bus." I grabbed her hand, and we flew down the hall like butterflies.

Author's Note

Like millions of children around the world, Lauren has ASD, also known as Autism Spectrum Disorder, which is an umbrella term that has included Asperger's since 2013. She experiences the world differently than other people—she has trouble reading facial expressions and tone of voice and understanding jokes.

These differences can make life challenging for people living with ASD, and for the people around them. However, it is these very differences that make them unique.

I've been a teacher for twenty years, and during that time I've been lucky enough to work with several students with ASD. They've taught me understanding and patience, and have helped me to see the world in a new way.

Thanks to: Gail Winskill, Ann Featherstone, and the team at Pajama Press for seeing a new and better way to tell this story; kc Dyer and the Surrey International Writer's Festival for your recognition of an early version of the manuscript; Stella Harvey, Rebecca Wood Barrett, Libby McKeever, Mary MacDonald, Sue Oakey-Baker, Katherine Fawcett, Nancy Routley, Lisa Richardson, and Pam Barnsley for your honesty, advice, and laughter; Norm, Johanne, Duane, Ben, and Julia for your love and support.